KT-436-894

This Little Tiger book belongs to:

Declan

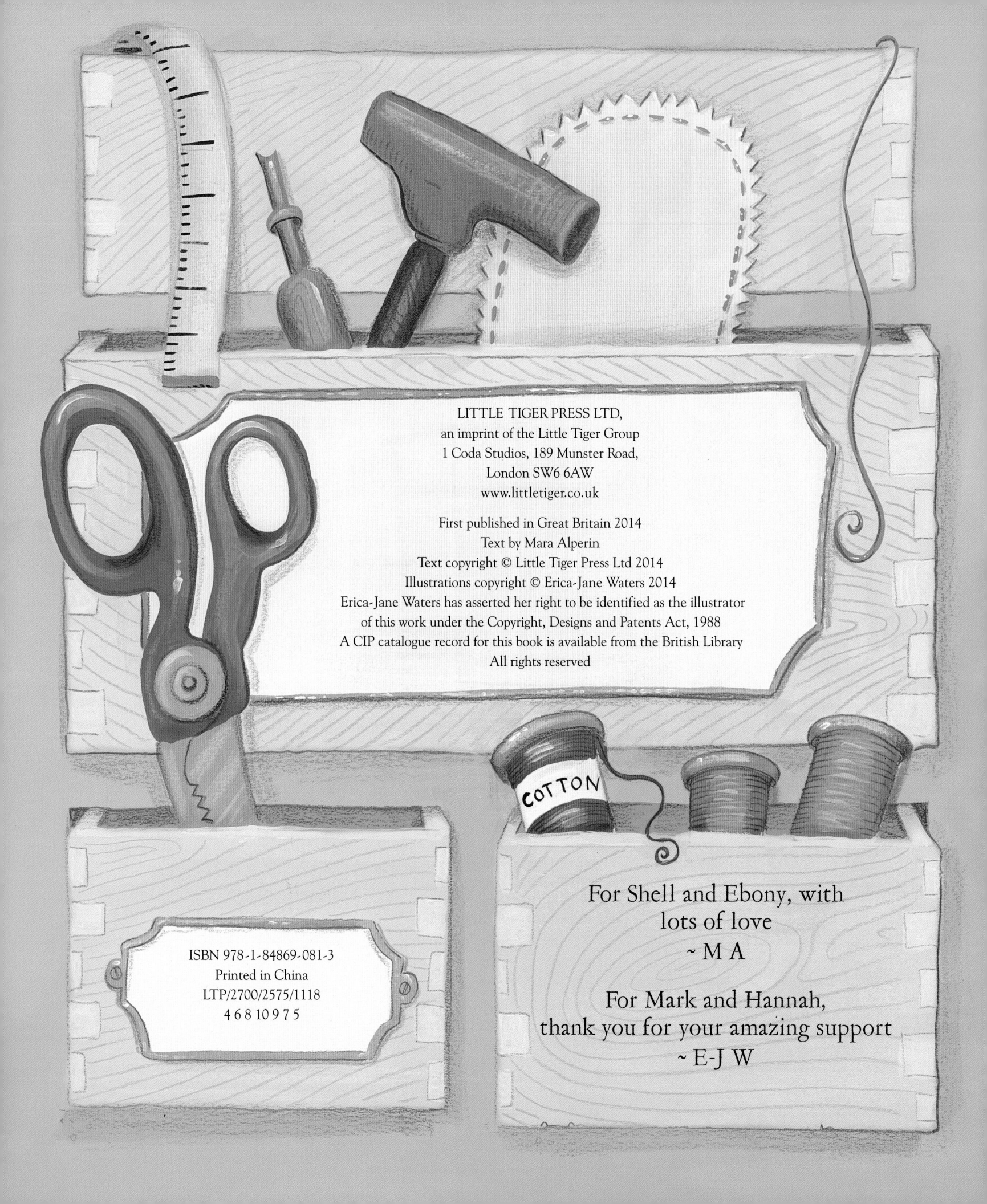

LITTLE TIGER PRESS LTD,
an imprint of the Little Tiger Group
1 Coda Studios, 189 Munster Road,
London SW6 6AW
www.littletiger.co.uk

First published in Great Britain 2014
Text by Mara Alperin
Text copyright © Little Tiger Press Ltd 2014
Illustrations copyright © Erica-Jane Waters 2014
Erica-Jane Waters has asserted her right to be identified as the illustrator
of this work under the Copyright, Designs and Patents Act, 1988
A CIP catalogue record for this book is available from the British Library
All rights reserved

ISBN 978-1-84869-081-3
Printed in China
LTP/2700/2575/1118
4 6 8 10 9 7 5

For Shell and Ebony, with
lots of love
~ M A

For Mark and Hannah,
thank you for your amazing support
~ E-J W

FAIRYTALE CLASSICS

The Elves and the Shoemaker

Mara Alperin

Erica-Jane Waters

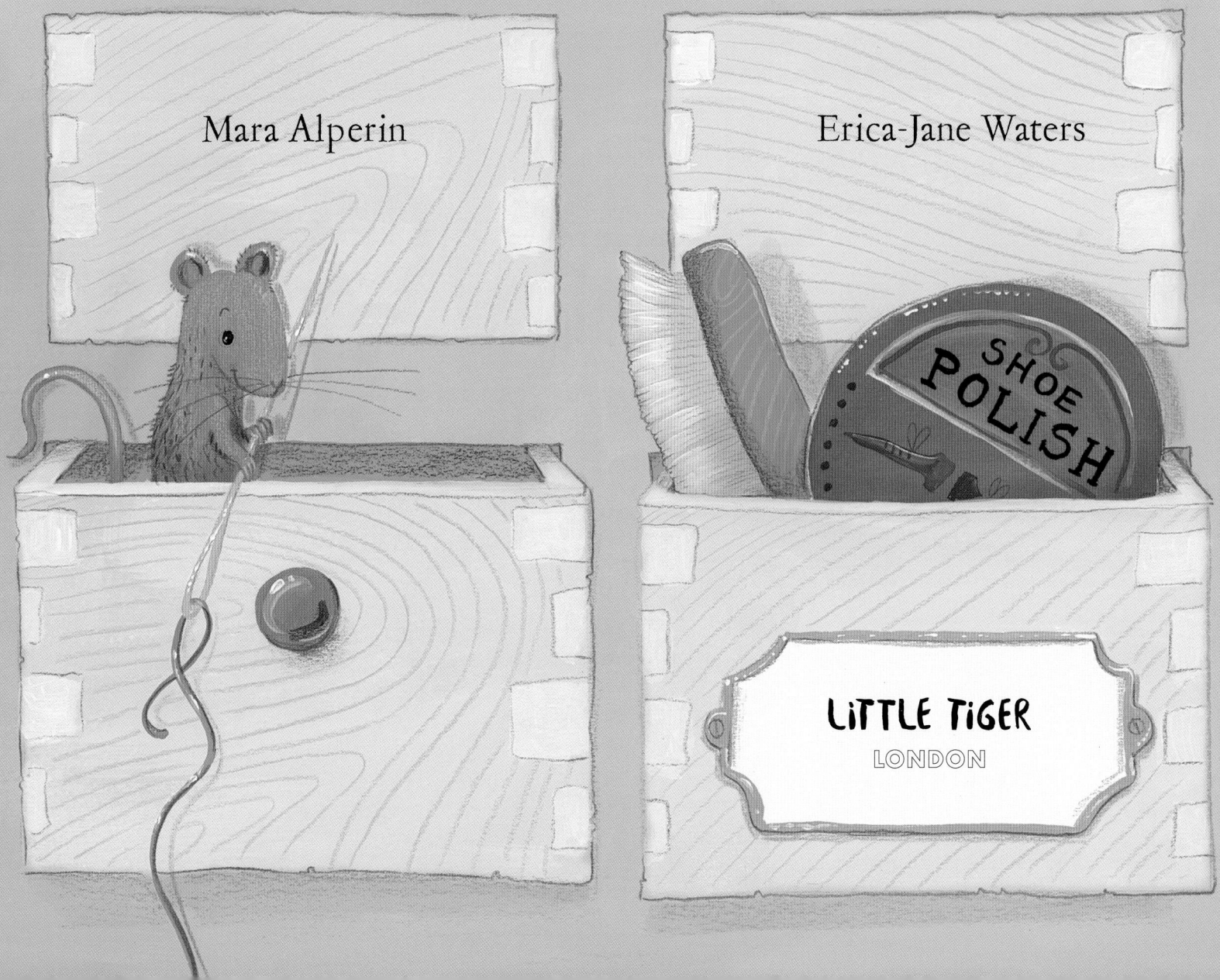

LITTLE TIGER
LONDON

In an old and shabby shoe shop,
there lived a cobbler, Stan,
and his wife, Jan.

Though they were poor, they were very happy,
for they loved to make shoes . . .
Shoes for walking and shoes for jumping, shoes for skipping . . .
and best of all,
shoes for
dancing!

Every day, Stan and Jan worked hard making shoes for their little shop . . .

and every evening, they slipped on their favourite dancing shoes and waltzed the night away.

The villagers loved to watch them dance,
and before long, people young and old **whirled**
and **twirled** through the door to join in.

All summer long the shoemakers danced,
sharing their joy with everyone around them.

But soon the bitter winter came.

And as the weeks passed, fewer and fewer customers stopped to buy shoes.

"Whatever will we do?" worried Stan. "Soon we will have **no** money left and **no** more firewood!"

The shop grew quieter . . .

and quieter . . .

That night, Stan and Jan huddled by the tiny fire, their fingers too cold to sew and their feet too frozen to dance.

"Let's g-g-go to b-b-bed," Jan chattered. "Perhaps we'll think of something in the morning."

But in the morning they awoke to find the most **magnificent** pair of shoes.

"**Leaping laces!** Who made these?" marvelled Stan.

Before they could start to wonder . . .

the shop door opened, and in marched their **first** customer in weeks.

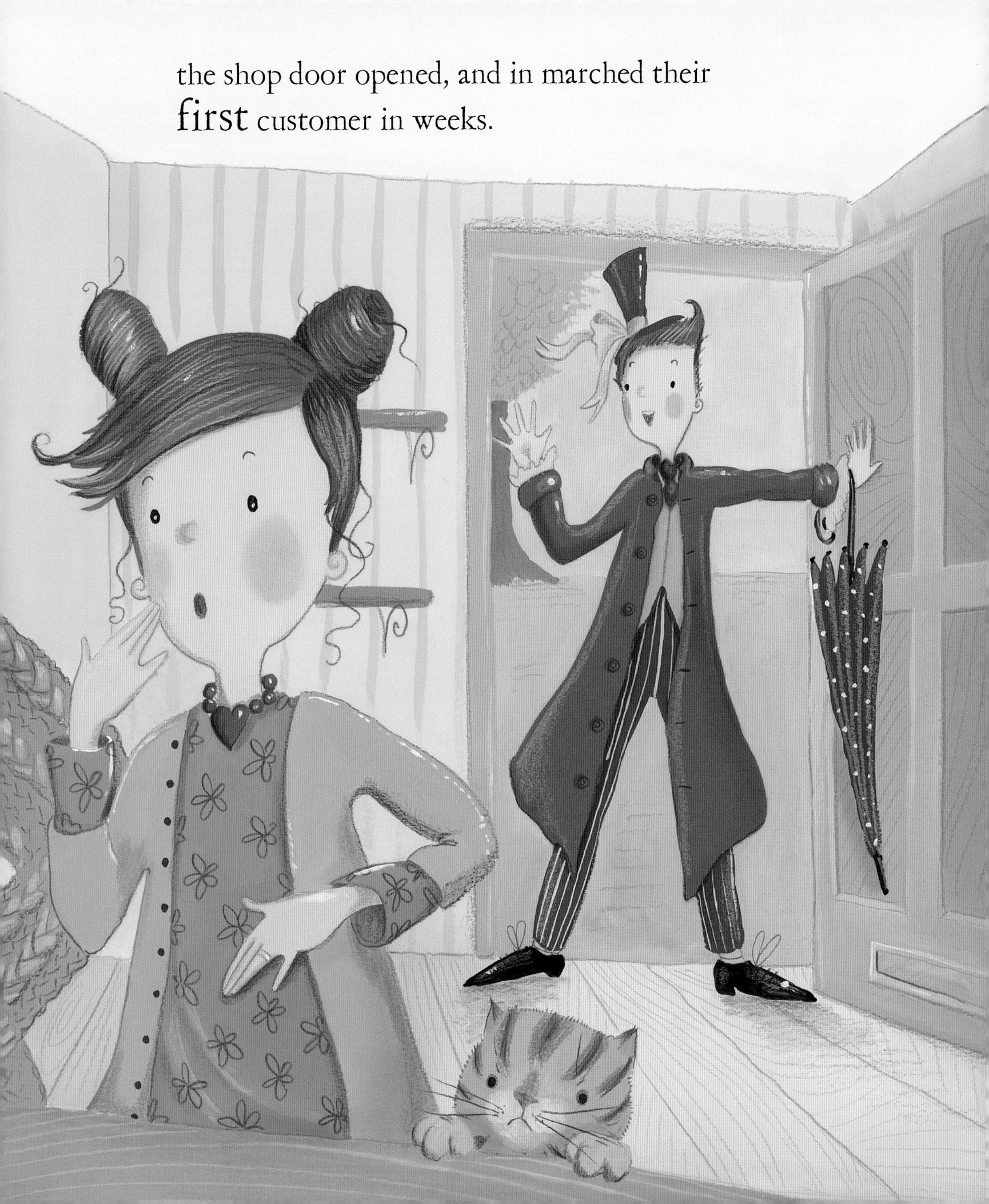

"Good day!" cried the customer.
"My name is Sir Flumby. I spied these
splendid shoes in the window
and I simply must have them!"

The shoes
fitted
perfectly.

So, Sir Flumby paid Stan a handful of gold pieces, and skipped away merrily in his new shoes.

Delighted, Stan went to the market to buy some supper and firewood.

And that night, the shoemaker and his wife danced with joy once more!

The next morning they found, to their amazement, **three** new pairs of shoes even more **stunning** than the last!

Stan and Jan could not believe their eyes! But just then . . .

"Greetings, Shoemakers! I am Sir Flipsy-Flopsy, and I have heard tales of your **marvellous** shoes."

"Why, they are even more fabulous than I imagined," he bellowed. "I shall buy them **all** – one pair for me, and the others for my horse, Toby."

So, Sir Flipsy-Flopsy filled the shoemakers' pockets with gold coins, and **galloped** off.

From then on, there were shiny new shoes **every** morning. Soon the shop was warm and cosy and bustling with customers day after day.

One day, Jan said, "We still don't know **who** is helping us. I wish we could thank them!"

Then Stan had a wonderful idea. "Why don't we stay up and find out?"

So that night, Jan and Stan hid behind the curtains. They waited, and **waited**, and **waited**...

until, as the clock struck **midnight**...

three tiny elves slipped in through the keyhole...

and tiptoed across the room!

The elves set to work with a stitch, stitch, stitch, and a rap-a-tap-tap. And as they worked, they sang:

We love jumping, leaping, prancing,
We were sad when you stopped dancing.
So in we creep while you are dreaming,
Making new shoes, bright and gleaming!

All night the elves sewed, until the sun began to rise.

And then quickly, quietly, they popped back through the keyhole.

Stan and Jan were so surprised by what they'd seen.

"What delightful little elves," Stan whispered. "We must repay their kindness."

"Let's make them their own little dancing shoes," said Jan. "And some dancing clothes, too."

So, the next morning, that's just what they did. Jan knitted tiny jumpers, using tiny pins . . .

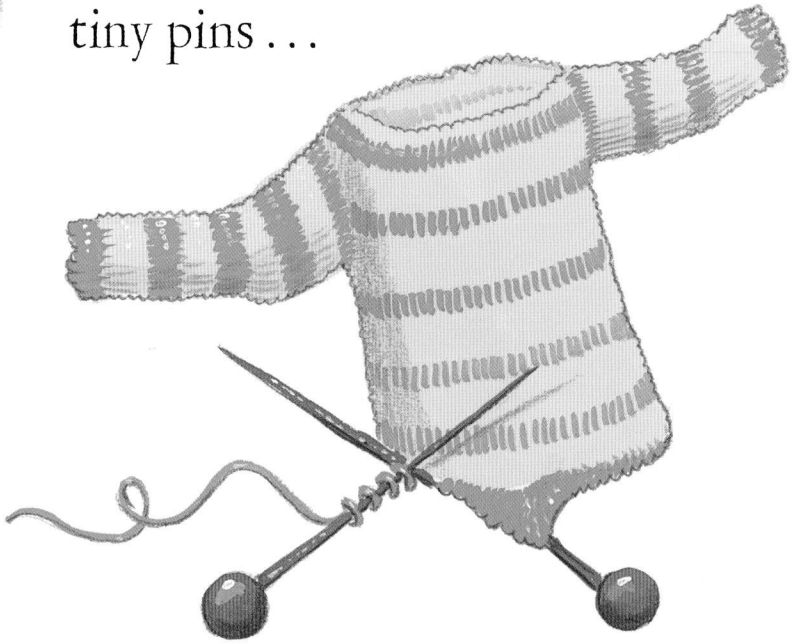

then sewed on tiny apple pips for decoration.

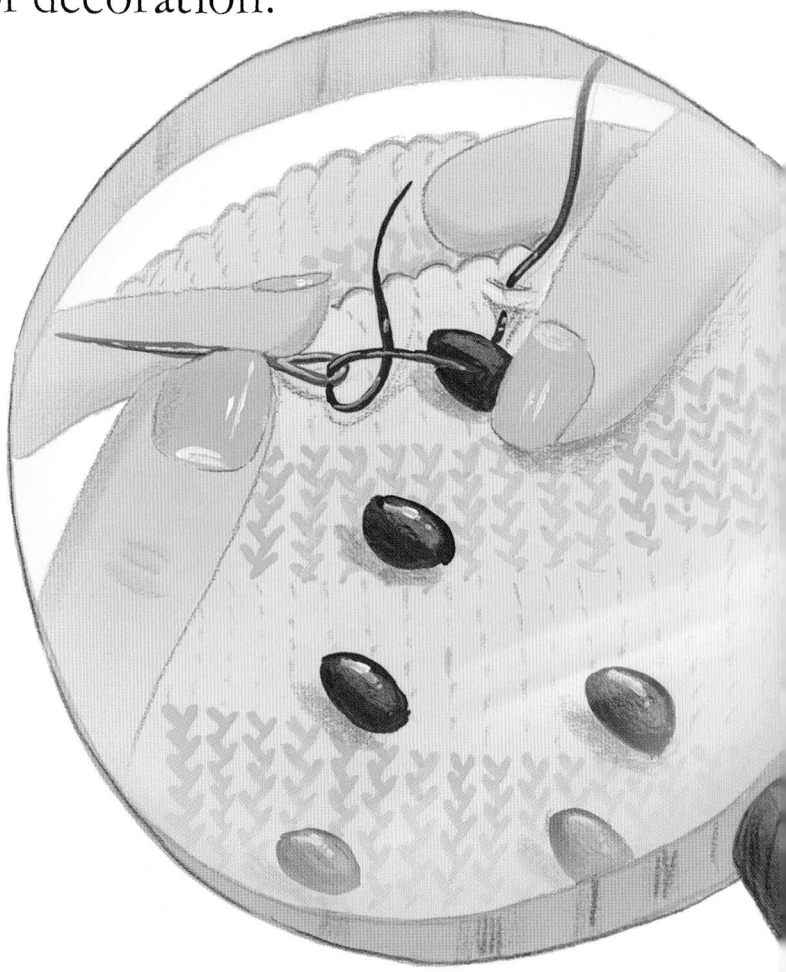

Stan crafted tiny shoes
from dandelion leaves . . .

then stitched them
with daisy stem laces.

And together they made little pointy hats,
finished with the tiniest pom-poms.

At midnight, Stan left the tiny parcel on the workbench, just before the three little elves crept inside.

When the elves saw their new clothes, they were overjoyed!

They giggled and wiggled,
and danced all night in
the moonlight.

But as the stars faded,
the three tiny elves
tiptoed away, and
vanished
into the night.

That was the last the shoemakers ever saw of the elves. But their kindness was never forgotten, and Stan and Jan danced **every** night with their friends just in case the elves ever returned.

And who knows . . . maybe
one day, they will!

FAIRYTALE CLASSICS

are familiar, fun and friendly stories –
with a marvellously modern twist!

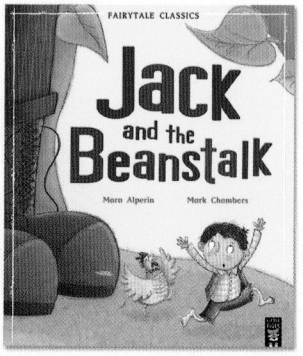